In loving memory
of Nanny and Grampa,
who always read
me poetry xx
L.R.

For Toni, Brian
& Sophie
N.R.

Bloomsbury Publishing, London, Oxford, New York, New Delhi and Sydney

First published in Great Britain in 2017 by Bloomsbury Publishing Plc
50 Bedford Square, London WC1B 3DP

www.bloomsbury.com

BLOOMSBURY is a registered trademark of Bloomsbury Publishing Plc

Text copyright © Lucy Rowland 2017
Illustrations copyright © Natasha Rimmington 2017
The moral rights of the author and illustrator have been asserted

A CIP catalogue record of this book is available from the British Library

ISBN 978 1 4088 5949 0 (HB)
ISBN 978 1 4088 5950 6 (PB)
ISBN 978 1 4088 5951 3 (eBook)

All papers used by Bloomsbury Publishing are natural, recyclable products made
from wood grown in well managed forests. The manufacturing processes
conform to the environmental regulations of the country of origin

Printed in China by Leo Paper Products, Heshan, Guangdong

1 3 5 7 9 10 8 6 4 2

Lucy Rowland   Natasha Rimmington

GECKO'S ECHO

BLOOMSBURY
LONDON OXFORD NEW YORK NEW DELHI SYDNEY

Once there was a gecko
and she lived inside a cave.
She was very **very** small
but she was also **really** brave.

GECKO'S CAVE

Her tail was long and flicky. She stood on four short legs,
and day and night she guarded her little gecko eggs.
She guarded them so carefully, she never turned her back.

You never know who's waiting for a tasty gecko snack!

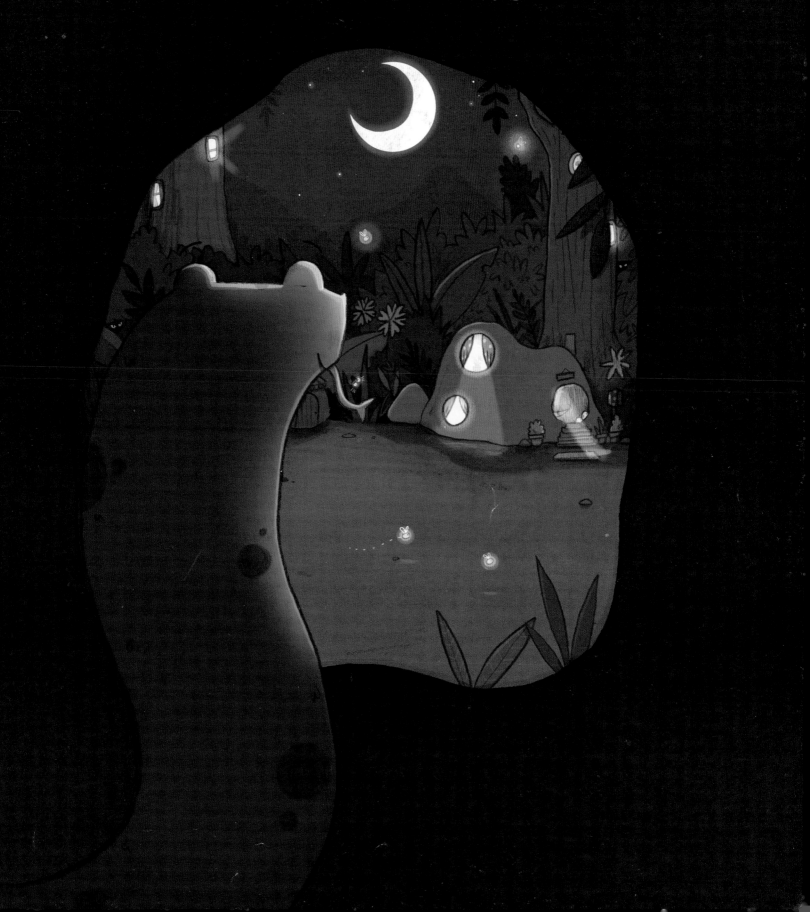

Early one hot morning, as the sun rose in the sky,
a snake spotted the gecko
as he slowly slithered by.

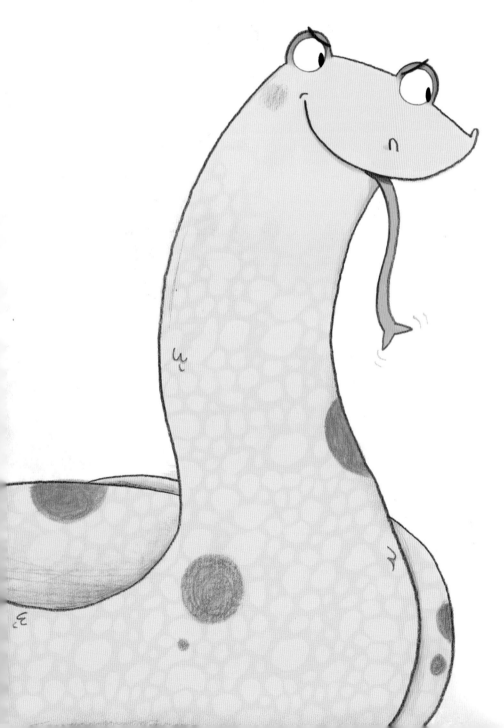

"Oh, Gecko,
what's inside your cave?"
said Snakey with a hiss.

"Mmmm, gecko eggs
for breakfast –
that's not something
I can miss!"

But Gecko turned to Snakey,

"Well, I hope you're feeling brave.

See, there's a hundred geckos

living right inside this cave.

If you're staying I can show you —
all it takes is one loud shout,
and a hundred angry geckos
will suddenly rush out!"

Snakey muttered crossly
then he quickly slid away.
"Those gecko eggs will have
to wait until another day."

Later that same morning,
when the sun was really high,
an eagle spied the gecko
as she circled in the sky.
"Oh, Gecko,
what's inside your cave?"
said Eagle with a smile.

"I haven't eaten gecko eggs
for lunch in quite a while."

"Well, Eagle," said the gecko.
"I just hope you're really fast.
I know a hundred geckos
and they'll never let you past.

If you're staying I can show you.
Just one shout, quite loud and clear.
And . . .

a hundred angry geckos

will suddenly appear!"

The eagle muttered crossly then she quickly flew away.
"Those gecko eggs will have to wait until another day."

But later in the evening as the sun
dropped through the sky,
a rat noticed the gecko
as he quickly scuttled by.

"Oh, Gecko,
what's inside your cave?
It's time for me to eat,
and gecko eggs for dinner
are my very *favourite* treat!"

Poor Gecko stood inside her cave.

"Stop!" she cried. "Beware!

A hundred geckos live in here.

Just try it if you dare!

If you're staying I can show you
with **one shout** into this cave.
They'll all be **very** angry so
I hope you're feeling **brave**."

But Rat wanted his dinner.
He licked his lips with glee.

"Why, yes I'm staying, Gecko,
and I'm having eggs for tea.

A **hundred** geckos living here?!
I **don't** believe it's true.
In fact," Rat said to Gecko,
"I'm **quite** sure there's only . . .

. . . YOU!"

"Suit yourself," said Gecko . . .

And she gave a mighty shout . . . .

" RAA

AAH!"

Then a hundred gecko voices suddenly boomed out.

"Uh oh! I think they're coming now!"
the clever gecko said.
Her little voice bounced round the cave
and echoed overhead.

"Yikes!" Rat said to Gecko and he scampered off so fast

that he didn't see the little gecko laughing as he passed.

Oh, how the gecko giggled as
she watched Rat run away.

"Well, fancy that," she laughed.
"My gecko echo saved the day!"

But as she crept along the rocks,
the gecko heard a

CRACK!

She shouted out,
"Oh, no! That nasty rat
is coming back!"

She rushed to guard her precious eggs then gave a little shout.

The eggs began to wobble, and three tiny heads popped out!

Proud Gecko grinned from ear to ear.
"You're here. You're safe," she said.

And later when the babies yawned,
she whispered, "Time for bed!"

At last, the gecko felt at peace.
The moon and stars shone bright.
She kissed each baby gecko and
she wished them all goodnight.